Max in the Jungle

Mary Hoffman

Illustrated by
John Rogan

Hamish Hamilton
London

For Laura Snow

HAMISH HAMILTON LTD

Published by the Penguin Group
27 Wrights Lane, London w8 5TZ, England
Penguin Books USA Inc., 375 Hudson Street, New York, New York 10014, USA
Penguin Books Australia Ltd, Ringwood, Victoria, Australia
Penguin Books Canada Ltd, 10 Alcorn Avenue, Toronto, Ontario, Canada M4V 3B2
Penguin Books (NZ) Ltd, 182–190 Wairau Road, Auckland 10, New Zealand

Penguin Books Ltd, Registered Offices: Harmondsworth, Middlesex, England

First published in Great Britain 1991 by
Hamish Hamilton Ltd

Text copyright © 1991 by Mary Hoffman
Illustrations copyright © 1991 by John Rogan

1 3 5 7 9 10 8 6 4 2

A CIP catalogue record for this book is available from the British Library

ISBN 0-241-13123-5

Set in 15pt Plantin by
Rowland Phototypesetting Ltd, Bury St Edmunds, Suffolk
Printed in Hong Kong by
Imago Publishing Ltd

Maxmin Salt whistled on his way home
from school. It was the last day of term and
the long summer holiday stretched before
him. Max was a Bodmin, one of the little
people who live behind the shelves and
under the counters of every supermarket.

Max's family lived in Seasonings, along with the Peppers, the Spices and the Hot-Chilli-Chutneys. As Max slipped into his home behind the shelf he sneezed as usual, as the spicy smells of Seasonings came to meet him.

"Atishoo!" he said loudly. "Hello Mum, I'm home."

Max's mum was looking at holiday brochures.

Max was dying to go Winter Sporting.
Bodmins can do that all year round, as long
as they can manage the journey to the
Frozen Foods section. There they have a
wonderful time after dark, when the
supermarket is closed, skiing down the
frozen peas slopes or climbing the
mountains of ice-cream boxes to go skating
at the top.

But Mrs Salt fancied the Grand Tour,
through the delicatessen counter.

8

"Imagine," she said, her eyes shining as she looked up from the brochure, "walking through the Black Forest Gateaux, visiting our cousins, the Dijon Mustards, and popping down to Bologna for a sausage! We might even get as far as the Chicken Kiev and the Russian salad!"

"I don't know," said Mr Salt. "Sounds a bit indigestible to me. I'd rather do a bit of wine-tasting over in the Off Licence."

Max was disgusted. "Is that all you can think of – eating and drinking?" he demanded. "I want to *do* something on my holiday."

Next morning Max got his wish. Uncle Mustard arrived unexpectedly. Montmin Mustard, known to everyone as "The Major", was a great explorer. He was full of exciting stories. He had explored right to the furthest corners of the supermarket but his favourite place was the Jungle.

"Ah, my boy," he said to Max. "You just haven't lived until you've seen the Jungle!"

"Can we, Mum?" said Max. "Can we have our holiday in the Jungle?"

"Of course, it is dangerous," said the Major, suddenly looking serious. "It's right by the entrance and the check-outs. There are Jumbos everywhere."

All Bodmins have to avoid being spotted by the big Jumbo-sized versions of themselves, who wheel their trolleys round the supermarket.

"That's right," said Max's mum. "I'm sure it's too dangerous."

"Not if we only travelled by night," pleaded Max.

Mr Salt was surprisingly keen on the Jungle idea.

"A Safari!" he said. "That *would* be a special holiday."

But what settled it was that the Major offered them his services as a guide.

They set off early next evening. Luckily it wasn't late-night shopping, or they wouldn't have been able to start till after half past eight. Even so, they had a five night march ahead of them.

They visited some interesting places on the way, like Bread and Cakes, where they met Max's schoolfriend Minmin Bap.

They even spent a day in Tea and
Coffee, which Max had learned about in his
history lessons. His teacher had told him
about the great Empress Tai-fou and her
English Ambassador, Earl Grey. He felt
quite at home among the dusty shelves as
he slept and sneezed the day away.

On the sixth night, they arrived suddenly
at the edge of the Jungle. Uncle Mustard
went first, then came back to tell them it
was safe.

"It doesn't *look* safe," thought Max.

Fighting their way through thick clumps of something labelled Devil's Ivy, the Major finally led them to a row of African violets where they made their first camp.

Trying to sleep on the hard ground, Max realised what the Major had meant when he said the Jungle was dangerous. Supposing a Jumbo wanted to buy an African violet? The Salt family could be revealed, camping behind it! Max glanced over to where his Uncle Mustard lay on his back snoring peacefully and felt comforted. The Major wouldn't let them down.

Max woke up next morning to his first day in the Jungle. It was unlike anywhere he had ever been – hot and damp and full of enormous leaves. Max was surrounded by thick green stalks and sudden vivid patches of colour that were sweet-smelling flowers.

That afternoon the Major took them on their first proper Safari. They had to crawl single file behind Red Dragon's Teeth plants to a grove of lilies. There Max couldn't believe his eyes when he saw a beetle bigger than his hand sitting on a leaf.

"A wild Red Leopard Bug," whispered the Major.

Just then an even larger creature, striped black and yellow, flew overhead.

"Splendid, splendid!" cried Uncle Mustard. "A Flying Tiger – very rare!"

In the days that followed Max saw many wonderful plants and creatures. The last day of the holiday started out as one of the best, when the Major took them to see the Big Caterpillars. They were amazingly large and furry and had so many legs that Max couldn't count them all.

It was on their way back to camp that
disaster struck. Mrs Salt stumbled over a
root and clutched at a large leaf. The leaf
buzzed and a small Flying Tiger leapt out
and stung her on the arm. The Major
bravely attacked it with his stick and it flew
off, but it was too late. Mrs Salt lay in the
peat, looking very pale. Mr Salt carefully
examined her arm and said there was no
sting left in it, but it was swelling up and
turning bright pink.

"If only we were back in Seasonings," Uncle Mustard groaned. "There's only one good cure for a Flying Tiger bite and that's vinegar."

The Major thought quickly.

"Max, your father and I will carry your mother to the edge of the Jungle. You must run to the nearest emergency point. I think there's one just over the border, in Fruit and Veg. Tell them what's happened and ask for some vinegar. Bring it back to us as fast as your legs will carry you. We'll be waiting in the Devil's Ivy."

Max ran, his heart pounding, over tangled roots and the edges of flower-pots, until he came out of the Jungle and into Fruit and Veg. He soon met another Bodmin as he crawled behind the marrows and was directed to an emergency point behind the carrots. He panted out his message and he was relieved to find they had some vinegar.

"You must be exhausted," said the medical Bodmin. "I'll take the liquid to your mother."

"No, no," shouted Max, struggling to his feet again. "I must go too."

The supermarket lights were already dimming by the time that Max and the doctor reached the Devil's Ivy. An anxious Uncle Mustard was looking out for them from the top of a Yucca. Mrs Salt was lying down, with her arm in a sling.

The doctor knelt down beside her and mixed a little of the vinegar with a handful of peat from the floor of the jungle. He rubbed it into her arm. Then he gave her a drink from a little bottle in his bag. Mrs Salt spluttered and sat up. She looked much better already.

They stayed on the edge of the Jungle for another two days, until Mrs Salt felt up to the return journey. By the time they got back to Seasonings, it was about a month since they had left their home.

"Ah!" said Mrs Salt. "Home, Savoury Home."

"Yes," said Mr Salt. "It's not to be sneezed at."

"ATISHOO!" said Max.